How the Camel got his Hump

Miles KeLLY

In the beginning of years when the world was new, there was **a camel.**

The camel did not want to work for the man like the other animals, so he lived in the middle of the Howling Desert. He ate sticks and prickles, and was most idle.

When anybody spoke
to him he said,

"Humph!"

Just 'Humph!' and no more.

On Monday the horse went to see the camel. The horse had a saddle on his back and a bit in his mouth.

He said, "Camel, come out and trot like the rest of us."

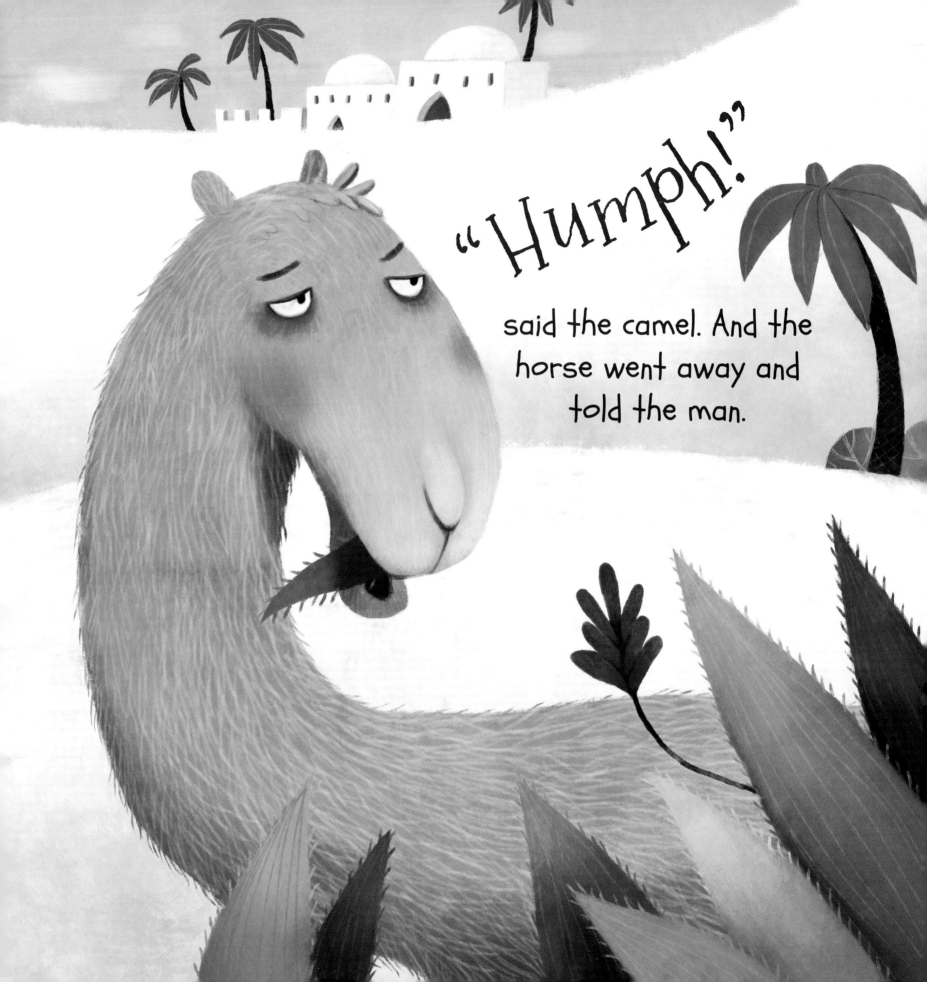

"Humph!"

said the camel. And the horse went away and told the man.

On Tuesday the dog went to see the camel. The dog had a stick in his mouth.

He said, "Camel, come and fetch like the rest of us."

"Humph!"

said the camel. And
the dog went away and
told the man.

On Wednesday the ox went to see the camel. The ox had a yoke on his neck.

He said, "Camel, come and plough like the rest of us."

"HUMPH!" said the camel. And the ox went away and told the man.

That evening the man called the horse and the dog and the ox together.

He said, "That camel in the Howling Desert won't work. You three must work double to make up for it."

That made the horse and the dog and the ox very angry. So they held a pow-wow on the edge of the desert.

The idle camel strolled by and laughed at them.

Then he said, "Humph!" and went away again.

So the three animals went to the genie in charge of all deserts and told him their problem.

The horse said, "There's an animal in the middle of your Howling Desert who is idle, and won't work."

"That's my camel!" said the genie in surprise. "What does he say about it?"

"He says 'Humph!'" said the ox. The genie flew off at once.

The genie found the camel being idle. "Camel, what's this I hear of you doing no work?" asked the genie.

"Humph!" said the camel. So the genie began to think a great magic.

"You've given everyone extra work ever since Monday, all on account of your idleness," the genie went on.

"Humph!"

said the camel. So the genie went on thinking a great magic.

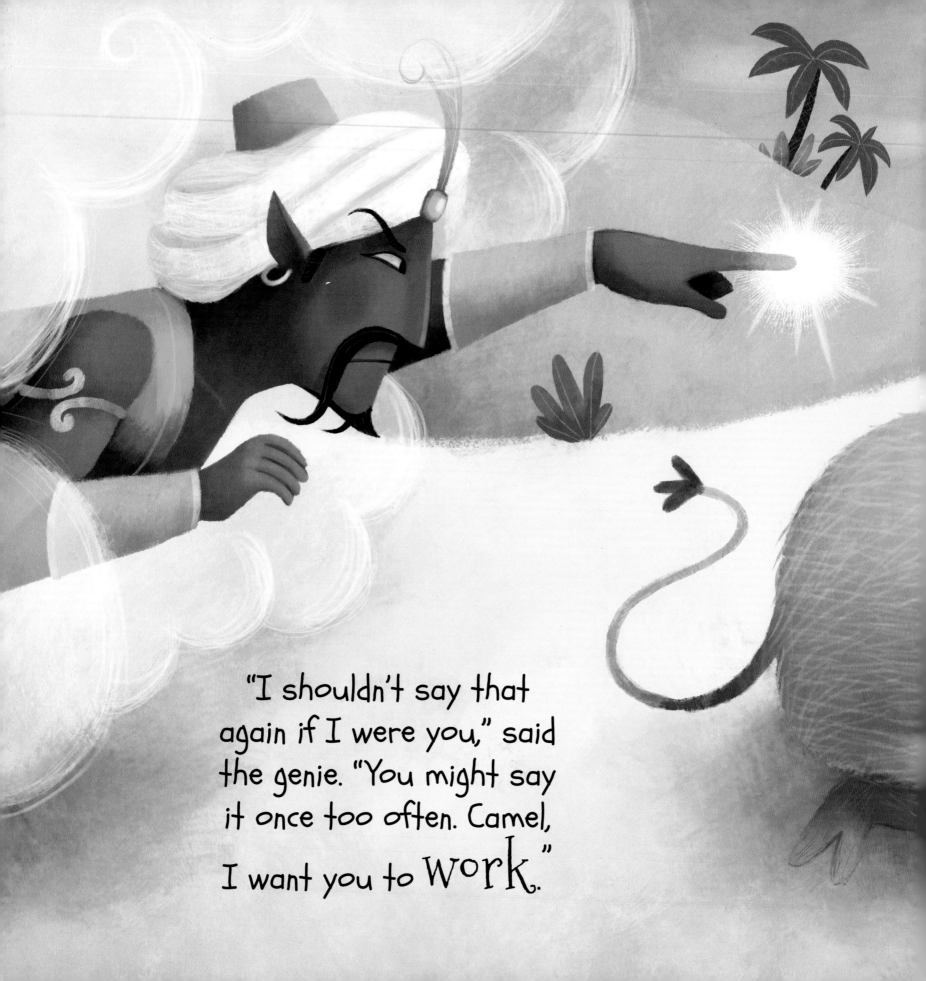

"I shouldn't say that again if I were you," said the genie. "You might say it once too often. Camel, I want you to work."

But the camel only said "Humph!" again.

No sooner had the camel said 'Humph!' a third time than his back began puffing up into a great big humph!

"There!" said the genie. "That's your very own humph that you've brought upon your very own self by not working."

"But how can I work with this humph on my back?" cried the camel.

"You would not work for three days. Your new humph lets you work for three days without eating," said the genie.

So the Camel humphed himself, humph and all, and went away from the Howling Desert.

And from that day to this, the camel always has a humph – but we call it a hump now, so as not to hurt his feelings.

But he has never yet caught up with the three days that he missed at the beginning of the world.

And he has never yet
learned how to behave.